Peter Rabbit

D1542537

Retold by
Sarah Toast

Cover illustrated by   Book illustrated by
Anita Nelson   Pat Schoonover

Based on the original story by Beatrix Potter with all new illustrations.

Louis Weber, C.E.O.
Publications International, Ltd.
7373 North Cicero Avenue
Lincolnwood, Illinois 60646

Manufactured in U.S.A.

8 7 6 5 4 3 2 1

ISBN: 0-7853-1144-0

PUBLICATIONS INTERNATIONAL, LTD.
Little Rainbow is a trademark of Publications International, Ltd.

#34244806

Once upon a time there were four little rabbits named Flopsy, Mopsy, Cottontail, and Peter. They lived with their mother in a rabbit hole under a very big fir tree.

"Now, my dears," said Mrs. Rabbit one morning, "you may go down the lane or into the fields, but don't go into Mr. McGregor's garden! He does not like little bunnies."

Then Mrs. Rabbit took a basket and set off through the woods for the baker's house.

Flopsy, Mopsy, and Cottontail were good little bunnies. They went down the lane to gather blackberries.

But Peter was very naughty. He ran straight toward Mr. McGregor's garden! When he got there, Peter squeezed under the wooden boards of the gate.

First Peter ate some lettuce and some green beans. Then he ate some radishes. And then, feeling rather sick, Peter went to look for some parsley to settle his tummy.

While Peter was out looking for parsley, whom should he meet but Mr. McGregor!

Mr. McGregor was down on his hands and knees planting cabbage. He jumped up and ran after Peter, waving a rake and shouting, "Stop, thief!"

Peter was awfully frightened. He rushed all over the garden, but he had forgotten the way back to the gate.

Peter lost one of his little shoes among the cabbage and the other in the potato patch.

After losing his shoes, Peter ran on four legs and went faster. He may have been able to escape altogether if he hadn't run smack into a gooseberry net. The large brass buttons of Peter's new jacket got caught in the net, and Peter tumbled over.

Peter had given up hope and shed big tears. Just as Mr. McGregor was marching up with a basket to plop on top of Peter, the bunny was able to wriggle out of his new jacket and get away from Mr. McGregor.

Peter rushed into the toolshed and jumped into a watering can that was near the door. It would have been a lovely place to hide in if it had not had so much water in it!

Mr. McGregor was sure that Peter Rabbit was hiding somewhere in the toolshed. He began to turn over every single flowerpot, looking for the naughty little rabbit.

Then, "Kertyschoo!" he sneezed, and Mr. McGregor was able to find Peter in no time.

Peter jumped out of a little window, knocking over three plants as he came through. The window was too small for Mr. McGregor to fit through, and he was tired of running after Peter. Mr. McGregor decided he would go back to his work.

Peter sat down to rest. He was out of breath and was feeling frightened. He had no idea how to find his way out of the garden. Peter Rabbit was also very wet from hiding in Mr. McGregor's watering can.

Peter wandered about, not going very fast, going lippity, lippity. He found a door in the garden wall, but it was locked and there was no room for him to squeeze under it.

A mouse was running in and out of the garden over the doorstep. She was carrying peas and beans to her family in the woods. Peter asked the mouse the way to the garden gate, but she had a large pea in her mouth and could not answer him. Peter began to cry again.

Suddenly Peter heard the scratching of Mr. McGregor's hoe. He climbed up on a wheelbarrow to get a better look.

The very first thing Peter saw was Mr. McGregor hoeing onions. Then he saw the gate beyond him!

Peter jumped off the wheelbarrow and started running as fast as he could, straight toward the gate. Mr. McGregor came running to catch him, but Peter slipped under the gate and was safe at last in the woods outside the garden.

Peter didn't stop running until he got home to the rabbit hole. He was so tired that he flopped down on the soft floor and closed his eyes. Mother Rabbit wondered what Peter had done with his little jacket and shoes.

Peter did not feel very well that evening. His mother put him to bed and gave him a dose of chamomile tea: "One tablespoonful at bedtime." But Flopsy, Mopsy, and Cottontail got to have bread and milk and blackberries for supper.

Mr. McGregor found Peter's little jacket in the gooseberry net and his little shoes among the cabbage and potatoes. He hung them up, making a scarecrow to keep the blackbirds out of his garden.